Tap it, tip ...

Written by Suzannah Ditchburn

Illustrated by Angelika Scudamore

Collins

Dad taps it.

Tap tap tap.

3

Dad tips it.

4

Tip tip tip.

Pat pat pat.

Tim sits.

Sit.

Sit sit sit.

Nap nap nap.

Tap, tap, tap.

12

13

14

After reading

Letters and Sounds: Phase 2

Word count: 36

Focus phonemes: /s/ /a/ /t/ /p/ /i/ /n/ /m/ /d/

Curriculum links: Understanding the World

Early learning goals: Reading: use phonic knowledge to decode regular words and read them aloud accurately; demonstrate understanding when talking with others about what they have read

Developing fluency

- Your child may enjoy hearing you read the book.
- Take turns to read the main text and Dad's speech bubbles. For pages 12 and 13, try out different voices for each character's speech bubble.

Phonic practice

- Turn to page 6. Ask your child to sound out the letters in each word, then blend. (T/i/m – **Tim**; p/a/t/s – **pats**)
- Challenge your child to read the whole sentence on page 6.
- Turn to page 4. Again, ask your child to sound out the letters in each word, then blend. (D/a/d – **Dad**; t/i/p/s – **tips**; i/t – **it**)
- Challenge your child to read the whole sentence on page 4.
- Look at the "I spy sounds" pages (14–15). Point to the igloo and say: "igloo", emphasising the /i/ sound. Ask your child to find more things in the picture that contain the /i/ sound. (e.g. *Tim, drink, biscuit, bin, window, picture, sill, sip, sink, igloo*)

Extending vocabulary

- Take turns to choose a command to read to each other. The listener has to follow the command in a mime.
  Tap it!   Tip it!   Pat it!   Sit!
- Take turns to point to a picture and say in your own words what the person or cat is doing. Choose the correct beginning to each sentence.
  Dad ...   Tim ...   The cat ...